Dogs and Bugs go together...really they do!

Penchina, Sharon.

Dogs and bugs go together-- really they do! / by Sharon Penchina & Stuart Hoffman.

p. cm. -- (I am a lovable me! ; 4)

SUMMARY: Collection of illustrated affirmations in rhyme format intended to teach children to express kindness, friendship and compassion in a world of diversity.

Audience: Ages 0-7.

ISBN-13: 978-0-9740684-8-0
ISBN-10: 0-9740684-8-9

1. Toleration--Juvenile literature. 2. Difference (Psychology)--Juvenile literature. 3. Interpersonal relations--Juvenile literature. [1. Toleration. 2. Prejudices. 3. Friendship. 4. Kindness. 5. Stories in rhyme.] I. Hoffman, Stuart, 1957- II. Title.

HM1271.P46 2006   179'.9
                                    QBI05-600200

2magine

Printed in China

Dogs and Bugs go together...really they do!

By Sharon Penchina C.Ht. & Dr. Stuart Hoffman

To my Angel~

Jasmine

2 Imagine

Scottsdale, Arizona

United States of America

Affirmations

I am a good friend.

I am calm.

I am patient.

I am very special.

I am thoughtful.

I am kind.

I am thankful.

I am open to new ideas.

I am adventurous.

I like going new places.

I like meeting new friends.

I am unique.

I am one-of-a-kind.

I am positive.

I encourage others to be positive.

I always shine from deep within.

I think happy thoughts.

I speak kind words.

I am joyful.

I am honest.

I am quite loyal.

I can be counted on.

My heart is filled with love.

I always lend a helping hand.

I am my own best friend.

Dogs and Bugs go together...really they do!

Part 4 of the

"I AM a Lovable ME!

Self-Empowerment series

In a world of diversity it is

love, kindness, and compassion

that must prevail.

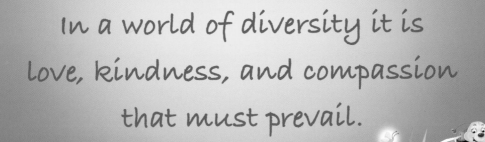

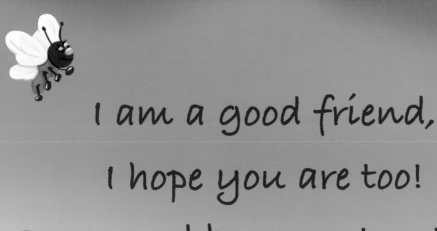

I am a good friend,
I hope you are too!
Dogs and bugs go together,
.....Really, they do!

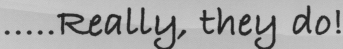

A bug can be quite loyal,
And be a dog's best friend.
I am calm, I am patient,
I will be there to the end!

I am very special,
And you are quite unique.
Is that your nose I'm looking at?
No, it's your beautiful beak!

I am thoughtful; I am kind,
To everyone I meet.
I always like to make new friends,
With or without feet.

Did you say, "Hippopotamus?"
That's an unusual name.
I am thankful for
your friendship,
And, I love you just the same!

I am open to new ideas!
Like swinging from tree to tree,
Or, buzzing like a Bee,
ZZZZzzzzzzzzzzzzzzzzzzzzzzzzzzzzzzzzzzzzzzzzzzzzzzzzzz

Or, moving slowly on the ground,

Or, spinning round and round and round.

I am adventurous.
I like going new places.
I love making new friends
Who have different faces.

I am unique,
I am one-of-a-kind.
One just like me?
An impossible find!

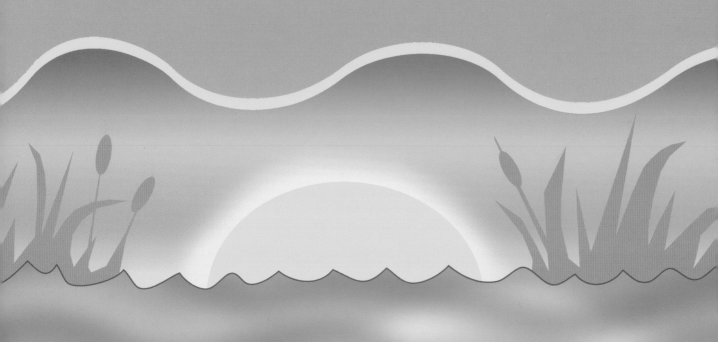

I am positive.
I encourage others to be positive, too!
I always shine from deep within.
It's who you are; not what you do.

I remember to be loving.
In what I say or do.
I think happy thoughts.
I speak kind words,

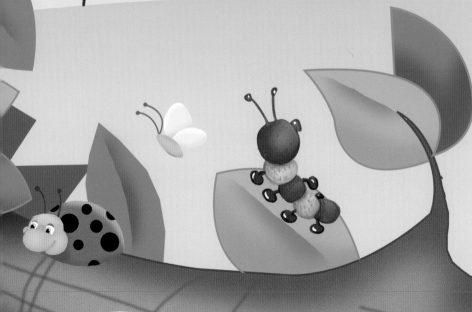

I am joyful
through
and
through!

I am honest.

I am quite loyal too!

You can rely on me.

I can be counted on,

As a friend who's

there for you!

My heart is filled
with love,
That I share with those I meet.

I always lend a helping hand.
My life is so complete!

When it comes
right down to it,

I am my own BEST FRIEND!
I'm there for me in every way,
On me I can depend!

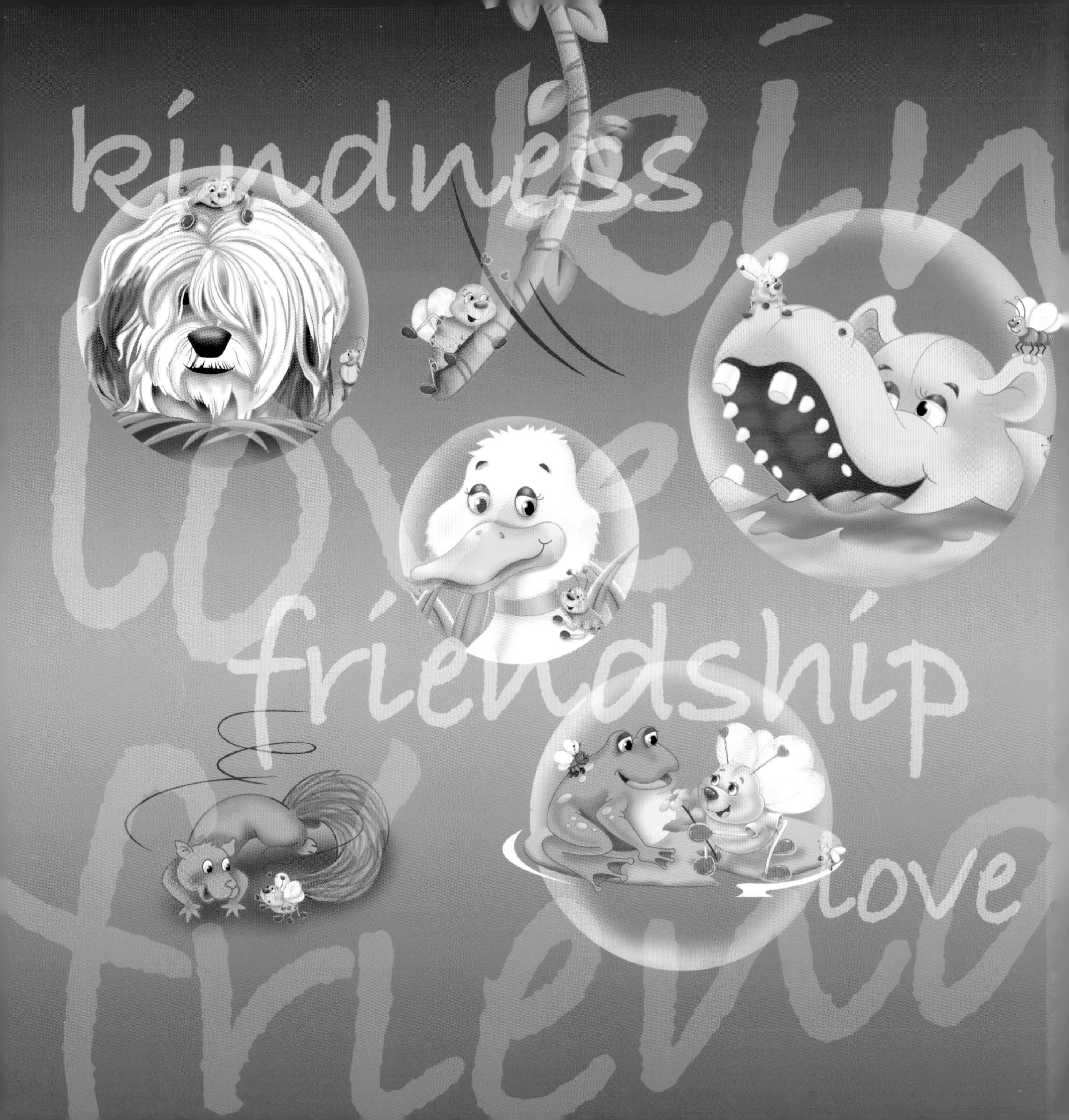
kindness
friendship
love